Chihuahua

CHIHUAHUA

ALEX THE BAND

Chihuahua

*Lyrics to the album
by
Alex the Band*

All Rights Reserved

Copyright © 2024 Alex Volz

This book may not be reproduced
in whole or in part without permission.

ISBN: 9798329470109

INTRODUCTION

This project took a long time to make. That's not the case for most of my projects. Most times they pop out in a fit of inspiration. But the length and breadth of this story meant I had to hack away at it for years.

Even before the hacking began, I was thinking about it. *Chihuahua's* climactic scene – the one involving an old man, his dog, and a passing train – was inspired by an Italian movie from the 50's named *Umberto D.* As far as I'm concerned, that scene is the closest any work of art has come to explaining the meaning of life.

I saw that movie once in the fall of 1999. *Chihuahua* was finished in the summer of 2024. So for that intervening quarter century, that idea lived in my imagination. I loved the story and its timeless message, but I didn't just want to rewrite *Umberto D* in a contemporary setting. I needed my own world, my own characters, and some unique take on the story that would justify its creation.

In the winter of 2021 I finally had an idea: instead of a book or a screenplay, I could tell the story of a man and his dog through a series of narrated songs. Just like a novel, I could use devices like changing perspectives, jumps in chronology, and the canvas of a large cast.

The idea finally clicked. I outlined a story, divided it into chapters and spent the next year writing and rewriting the lyrics and music several times. In February 2023, I performed the first version of Chihuahua for my band.

Understandably, they were somewhat perplexed.

We just spent the last year recording a good time rock album, and this new project was long and slow and depressing and definitely not rock. They were good sports about it — even when my ideas for the music were terrible.

At first I wanted it to sound like *Views*-era Drake, with moody synths and atmospheric beats that evoke the feeling of an empty city at night. At one point I tried developing some chapters in the style of Huey Lewis and the News. I toyed with the idea of making samples from recorded city sounds. I had plans to use a Shepard's tone. For *Chihuahua*, the journey from vague idea to finished project was a long and stupid one.

I had always planned on adding more instruments and developing a fuller symphonic sound, whatever that would be. I even recorded a full version of the album in the summer of 2023 with the plan to add more instruments. But once I started performing *Chihuahua* live as a solo act with me and my guitar, I realized I didn't need any other instruments. So I threw out the album I just spent months recording, and decided to start again.

But first I just wanted to play it live for a while. I learned how to let the tempo of the music rise and fall with the pace of the story. I learned how to let the music breathe and how to play the silences. I found some useful moments of levity. And mostly, I just found confidence with the project.

In June 2024 I went into the Soundry in scenic Soddy Daisy, Tennessee. Two hours later, I walked out with a finished album. I played the first chapter a couple of times, but other than that the whole album was all recorded live in one take. I feel like Brettt Nolan did a great job of capturing the energy and feel of a live performance, and I love how you can hear the sound of me holding my breath as I play the trickier guitar parts.

It was a strange feeling walking out of the studio that day. After that story had lived in my imagination for a quarter century, I finally felt like I'd let it out. But even with all that planning and writing and rewriting and live rehearsing, I was still revising and making changes on the fly as we recorded it in the studio that day.

So even though the album's been recorded and released, *Chihuahua* will probably continue to grow and evolve as it enters this next phase of its life. Whatever that may be.

-Alex

Chapter 1: The Apartment

The old man and the old woman
Were holding hands as they went looking
For a new place they could call home.
They were hoping they could stay in the same zip code
But they stopped cold at the train stop
They saw an ambulance and a couple cops
They turned the lights on and they drove off
The old man wondered what was going on.

They kept going on slowly passing
A bench where a couple teenagers were laughing
The old man asked and so they explained
How they just saw somebody get hit by a train.
The old man asked the punk kids
Was he pushed into the tracks or did he jump in?
The kids just laughed and said it didn't matter.
There was a stain on the tracks where somebody had splattered.

There was a shopping cart that had been upended
A bunch of old junk that had once been in it,
And whoever had died had just been alive,
And pushed everything that he owned inside,
And the grisly sight of that greasy stain
Kept replaying in the old man's brain

For the rest of the day with the old lady
As they searched apartments that had been vacated.

The leasing agent smiled politely
As she opened the door and she warmly invited
The old couple into the new remodeled
Two bedroom former tenement apartment.
It was the same kinda building that had always been
In the same neighborhood where they had always lived
But the old man thought he must have gone crazy
When he heard rent quoted by the leasing agent.
So he asked her to repeat it cuz he must be mistaken.
That was three times the rent they were currently paying.
But the leasing agent told him times have changed,
You're paying for the things that make the neighborhood great.
Like the vegan restaurants and the coffee shops,
Where you can get out of your house and work on your laptop.
But the old man didn't have a computer.
He still bought some pieces of paper when he wanted to read the news,
And he drank the kind of coffee that Mr. Coffee brewed,
And he never met a vegan that he personally knew
And all over town he heard the same thing:
"Sorry old man but your neighborhood's changed
There ain't nothing even close to that price range,
Have you thought about a neighborhood that's farther

away?"
But some things are easier said than done
Like leaving the neighborhood that you know and you love.

So the old man and the old woman
Were still holding hands, but they quit looking,
And they walked home at the end of the day
Where they could hear that sound from several blocks
away….

It was the barking of their little Chihuahua.

Chapter 2: The Chihuahua

The old man never wanted that chihuahua
But it did not matter what the old man wanted
He didn't want the pooping or the barking
He was happy in his quiet little apartment
But he knew the choice had already been made
So he never tried to argue or complain
When he wife returned from the market one day with
A little lost chihuahua wrapped inside a blanket.

So for years he took that chihuahua out for walks,
When it was raining, freezing cold, or blazing hot.
And he learned to love its yippy little barks
And to tolerate all those chihuahua farts
Because he knew how happy that dog made his wife,
And how it gave some purpose to her life,
And how it made their apartment feel just like a home,
And how they never could have children of their own,
And so they never had some grandkids to distract 'em
From the scenery of life that keeps on moving past 'em.

And so he put up with the pooping and the barking
They could hear from blocks away as they came walking
Through the neighborhood and the dog could smell 'em,
And he'd commence his symphony of yelping
And that's sound the old man heard today

As hand-in-hand the couple made their way
Back to their apartment once again
After searching for a new place they could live.
But they couldn't find a place they could afford
After 30 years of living rent controlled
And 30 days since the present landlord
Told them all the houses on the block were sold.
And as he as he opened the door and let it swing wide
That happy little chihuahua jumped up to say hi.
And the old man thought about how strange it all felt
To know they'd soon be coming home somewhere else.

Chapter 3: The Old Man

The old man had been many things in his life.
He'd been a soldier, he'd been a husband, and now he was retired.
And he'd worked a bunch of jobs for the last 70 years,
But it was nothing that really added up to what you'd call a career
If it needed to be done, he'd be down to do it.
Sometimes he'd get hurt but he'd muscle through it.
She'd say see a doctor, but he'd swear he'd be okay,
Besides, he already had work lined up for the next day.
And some under the table cash helped to supplement
Their social security disability payments.
Now they didn't have much, but it was enough to get by,
And as long as the rent was controlled,
He could consider himself retired.

So the old woman's heart quietly broke
As she packed his lunch bag, and he went looking for work.
He climbed on the bus, and he rode back to the place
Where he'd score some odd jobs in his younger days.
It was the place folks went to rent moving trucks
And they'd hire some guys for a few extra bucks.
And those younger guys all looked so surprised
When the bus doors opened, and the old man arrived.
They were happy to get to see their old friend again,

But sad to hear about his apartment predicament.
And even though he was old and couldn't carry much weight,
They were happy to help him find some work for the day.
They'd carry the furniture and let him box the shelves,
And at the end of the day they paid him the same as they paid everybody else.
Because they loved that old man and were happy to repay him,
For when he scored the jobs and it was him paying them.

The old man was tired, but he was grateful for work,
And was grateful to find himself a seat on the bus.
And he longed for the bed he knew was awaiting,
As he heard that barking from several blocks away.
But there was a panic in that little dog's yelp
Something was wrong, and the dog needed help.
And as he opened the door, and let it swing wide
He prayed to God as he looked inside…

Chapter 4: The Old Woman

A comet struck the old man's world.
He struggled but he couldn't find the words
When the EMTs asked if there was anything he needed
Before they loaded up and started leaving.
But with everything he needed in that moment
'Nothing' was the only thing he told 'em.
The sirens wailed and colored lights were flashing
Reflections dying out as they drove past him

So he walked back to an apartment that was empty
Except for the chihuahua that was screaming.
Screaming for how long he couldn't say,
He remembered coming home from work that day,
And his pace grew quicker as he reached the door
And he found his wife unconscious on the floor.
He fell right there beside her, tried his hardest to revive her,
Called for help but felt no life inside her.

The defibrillator made her body shake,
But everybody knew they were too late.
All the while the doggie barked and barked,
But the old man could only hear his thoughts.
Then just as quick the chaos disappeared,
And that barking was all that he could hear.
With all the tragedy the old man had suffered,

He remembered he forgot to feed it supper.

So he scooped out some kibble, and scooped out some more,
And the dish overflowed and it spilled on the floor.
And though he was hungry, that doggie would not dine,
Not while the old man had tears in his eyes.
So he hopped into the old man's lap,
And nestled in the old man's hands,
And he searched for a way without words he could say,
That they'd both live to see another day.

Chapter 5: Alone

The old man didn't want to leave the chihuahua alone.
The old man didn't want to leave his home.
But the list of things to do kept piling up
So he walked to train station about a half a mile up
And he could still see that greasy stain
Where a homeless man was run over by a train.
The old man kept on walking and tried to forget it.
Paid his fare and the machine printed a ticket.
He found a seat and made his way downtown,
And squeezed through many busy sidewalk crowds.
Until at last he made it all the way
To the office to apply for Section 8.
And he waited there for hours all alone,
In a lobby full of people looking at phones,
And then worker finally came and called his name and
Thanked him for having so much patience.
She typed in her computer as she asked him,
Questions like his name and current address,
And income status and any family that might one day share the place,
And the old man opened up the floodgates

He told her how the neighborhood was sold,
And now all the neighbors had just 30 days to go,
And how it was hard enough to find a place to live in,

But his wife had died and he lost her social security benefits.
And then one day a friend at work had told him,
How Section 8 had apartments he could afford and,
So he left his grieving chihuahua all alone,
Because this was their only chance to find a home.

And the overworked girl behind the computer
Tried her best to sound reassuring
As she told him she'd add his name to the list
And when it was his turn, somebody would call him.
And naturally he asked her how long that would be,
And she said she couldn't say with certainty.
So he asked her how many names on the list preceded him
And she told him there were 973 of them.
So the old man told her how in a couple weeks,
He'd have no choice but live out on the streets,
And he wouldn't have a phone to call even if
972 names suddenly vanished from her list.

The young woman typing behind the computer
Could not count all the times that she'd been through this.
It broke her heart to hear stories like his,
And she resented the implication that she was cool with it,
Like there was something to be done, if she'd do it,
But that for some cruel reason she was refusing,
She felt that he'd been rude and so in turn,
She shared her thoughts and did not hold her tongue.
She said she'd love to help, but she ain't the mayor.

Unlike Jesus she ain't nobody's savior.
She ain't got no presidential powers,
She types types names on a list for 13 bucks an hour,
And should any of those names ever get a place,
It's not like they'll ever call her to say thanks.

In his desperation the old man started pleading.
He raised his voice and it sounded like he was screaming.
A security guard popped his head over her shoulder,
To make sure everything was still kosher.
The old man told him everything was fine
He stood up to go and thanked them for their time
And he didn't make a peep as he walked out
And merged with all the busy sidewalk crowds.

His feet were moving slow but his mind was racing
As he slowly made his way back to the train station.
He reached into his pocket and counted quarters to burn while,
He watched a group of teenagers jump the turnstile.
The old man knew he needed every single cent,
If he ever hoped to afford a new apartment,
And to be honest it made him feel like a stooge,
To be the only one following all the rules,
When doing so had only put him in the place,
Of desperation where found himself today.
So he kept his quarters clinched tight in his fist,
And past the turnstile the old man slipped.

And for the first time in at least a couple days,
The old man felt something other than grief and pain.
He felt some tiny measure of control as,
The train doors opened, and the old man boarded.
And as he took his seat he felt strangely proud
That he didn't let the turnstyle push him around.
Maybe just this once, in just this one tiny way
He'd have some hand in controlling his fate.
And he rode that cloud for one short moment,
Until they reached the next train station, and the train doors opened.
And there among the people getting on and off,
Were a couple uniformed metro cops.

"Show your tickets please," they told all the crowd
Who did just as instructed and held their tickets out.
And the metro cops passed between the aisles
Inspecting every ticket with a friendly nod and a smile.
The old man's heart was on a roller coaster,
As one by one the metro cops got closer.
Then one cop stopped beside some homeless man,
Who was drunk and passed out and had pissed his pants.
Now to metro riders on their daily commutes,
It was an everyday horror to which they'd grown immune.
But the metro cop demanded the homeless guy's ticket,
As if there was a chance in hell that he'd get it.
So instead of getting a ticket, both cops got both his middle

Fingers, screaming, cussing, spittle.
And the old man watched and said a silent prayer
To thank God for putting that homeless guy there.
And the old man happily watched as the metro cops
Dragged the homeless man off at the next train stop.

And he kept on counting his blessings as he went walking
Back to his soon-to-be-demolished apartment.
When he noticed a sound that he wasn't hearing…
There was no chihuahua barking in the distance to greet him.

Chapter 6: A Grand Adventure

The Chihuahua knew that something was amiss
When the old lady never came back to the apartment.
The old man sat and cried for days and days.
The chihuahua told him to be strong and be brave.
Not with words he said but things he did
Like hugs and snuggles and lots of licks.
And the dog could tell it helped the old man's hurting,
But it did not help the old woman's returning.

But the chihuahua knew that's what would be required
If he had a chance to stop the old man's crying.
So when the old man finally went out for the day,
The chihuahua found a way to do the same.
He hopped up on the back of the commode,
Where a tiny little window was left open.
The chihuahua always knew that he could do it
He just never had a reason to jump through it.
All his needs were met within these walls.
Destiny was set within these walls.
Questions never stretched beyond these walls.
Threatening worlds existed out beyond these walls.

To a chihuahua death does not exist,
So he knew that he'd find her if he just persisted.
And he trotted along for hours smiling,

Certain that any minute he would find her.
And he found a lot of stuff while he was out on his great big walk.
And everything that he saw deserved a great big bark.
Because the world can seem scary when you're only six inches high,
And you need to believe you can take any fight.
So he tried to look tough, but he just looked adorable,
And everything he barked at just ignored him,
And every time that they did and kept walking by him,
He assumed that his barking had worked, and he had frightened 'em.

And never did find that the old woman, but he did soon discover
A ravenous chihuahua-sized hunger.
So he looked around, and he realized he had no clue
Where he was, or how would get any food.
The Chihuahua was lost but he was not alone
He turned to see that he was being followed…

Chapter 7: A Desperate Search

Block by block the old man walked as fast as his legs would allow.
He whistled and he kissed and called his lost dog's name out loud.
And every passing stranger saw the panic in his eyes,
And they hoped the old man found his dog before disaster strikes.

But despite the old man's searching, the chihuahua couldn't be found.
It got dark and he got tired so he went home and he laid down.
And he let his tired feet rest but he couldn't rest his mind
Because he couldn't find his dog, and he would never find his wife.
And that loneliness it crushed him until he couldn't breathe,
And as soon as the morning sun came up he was back out on the streets.
He slammed the door behind him, and in his rush ignored,
The eviction notice that someone had tacked to his front door.

He walked his neighborhood in wide concentric circles,
Calling to his lost dog, and praying he'd be heard but,
The dog never came running and so the old man had no

choice,
But to walk until his feet were sore and yell until he was hoarse.
Maybe death and housing were problems he couldn't solve,
But at least for now he held out hope that he might find his dog.
But with every passing day, the old man's hopes grew dimmer,
And eviction notices blew off of his door and turned to litter.

He was driven by the thought of how scared his dog must be
To have no home to sleep in and to have no food to eat.
They were all the the same basic fears that he felt about himself,
But he put them in the dog and saving him became the quest.
But the old man didn't have the strength to gaze into that mirror,
And thought that if he whistled louder, the dog would surely hear him.
And when his feet could walk no more, he sat upon the shady grounds of
Some three-story luxury condos, and he whistled even louder.
A security guard heard him and felt it was his duty,
To politely suggest the old man stand and keep on moving.
And in those precious moments before and argument could

erupt,
The old man heard salvation in the window up above…

Chapter 8: The Young Man

Once upon a time there was a young man and his wife.
They had a child and bought a home for the first time in their lives.
It was a modest three story condo in a neighborhood that was rapidly changing.
There was still some poverty but plenty of places that were great.
Like the vegan restaurants and the coffee shops,
Where he could get out of his house and he could work on his laptop.
And sure it was farther out than where they had been living,
They loved their old neighborhood, but those rent hikes were unforgiving.
And it's true a three story condo wasn't exactly what they envisioned,
When they pictured the first home, the family who'd live in it.
They'd pictured a big backyard with a hammock in the shade,
Where a man and his best friend could spend their dog days.

But the cost of city living forced them both to compromise,
And so they bought themselves a condo when they had themselves a child.
And they still saw the occasional homeless guy out their on

the street,
And they hated the reminder that other people were in need,
But they knew there was only so much good that two people could do,
They shared all their spare change, and the same with their clothes and shoes,
And they sent donations to respectable causes,
And voted for politicians with respectable promises,
And they tried their hardest to show patience and empathy
For all those lost souls left out on the streets.

Like just the other day the young man was out walking
Their son in a stroller when he heard this yippy barking.
It was a frightened little chihuahua, lost and all alone.
It was hungry, it was trembling, and in need of a loving home.
So he took a fuzzy blanket from the baby carriage,
Wrapped that chihuahua in it, and he carefully carried him,
Home to his condo and introduced him to his wife,
Who reminded him of the non-existent yard they had outside,
And the baby's still so young, and their time is so limited.
Would they even have enough free time to spend with it?
It was a mild protest. Her heart wasn't in it.
When she saw how much he loved that dog, she knew she'd soon live with it.

And so their family of three became a family of four,

And all the chihuahua's needs were once again provided for.
And though that doggie was so grateful for how generous they'd been,
He'd sit and watch the window hoping to see the old man again.

Chapter 9: The Reunion

And that brings us back to where we had been
When the old man heard his dog barking at him again,
And he looked up at the window there above him,
And saw the only thing on Earth that loved him.
Then the door opened up, and the little doggie ran,
And leapt into the old man's waiting hands,
And the young man watched the two were united,
And in that moment the young man decided,
That the little homeless dog already had a home,
And it wasn't his three story condo.

He was sad to lose the dog, but even greater,
To lose the future memories he'd been making.
So now he'd scrap his plans and start again,
Imagining a man and his best friend.
And the old man was so happy and excited,
He forgot to ask the young man for a ride back home.
He started walking just as happy as could be.
He didn't even think about the blisters on his feet.
And he rode that happy cloud for several blocks,
But when he saw it he abruptly stopped…
Jaw dropped,
Shocked and aghast.
The reality he'd been avoiding,
Suddenly came crashing back.

Chapter 10: The Shopping Cart

He saw a chest of drawers his father made and then,
Checked the drawers and found his underwear within.
The bed and all the bedding where he'd planned to sleep,
Were resting in the yard for everyone to see.

A pile of family faces looking back from all
The family photographs that used to line the walls.
Silverware, dishes, and a pile of shoes,
Refrigerator full of his expired food.

From great to small he saw it all out in the yard:
Record player, kitchen table, kibble for the dog,
A couple empty shelves with all the books beside,
The plants his wife had watered when she was alive.

A life of artifacts collected on the way,
Locked in his apartment where they should be safe,
But those eviction notices were on the door,
Warning this would happen, but they were ignored.

Until he found it all scattered in the yard,
It was more than he could carry so he found a shopping cart,
He salvaged what he could, all the things he knew he'd need.

And saved a couple extra things with sentimental meaning.

He took some socks and shoes and some underwear to change,
The lock box in his desk with the little cash he'd saved
He grabbed a couple albums full of faded family photos,
Took the dog food and grabbed the water bowl.
And up on top it all the little doggie hopped
and the old man pushed the cart
Until they disappeared into the dark.

Chapter 11: Goodbyes

The young man was just minding his own on the steps of his three story condo
Warm night, cool beer; something in the air felt wrong though.
His wife and his kid were sleeping, but his mind was too restless to rest.
He was thinking about the chihuahua, and he knew it worked out for the best,
But he couldn't deny how lonely it felt to be there all alone,
And how much nicer it'd be right now with a chihuahua to hold.
Then heard and rattling clatter approaching block by block
And from the darkness came an overflowing shopping cart.

The young man was annoyed his peace had been disturbed
And briefly reconsidered the virtues of living in the suburbs.
So he finished the last of his beer and turned to go back in,
When he could have sworn he heard that chihuahua barking at him again.
So he turned back around, and chihuahua perched up on top
Of the junk that filled some poor homeless guys shopping cart.
The young man was overjoyed to see that chihuahua again,
But was surprised to see that the old man was the homeless

guy pushing him.

So he reached into his pockets to find him some spare change,
But the old man waved him off. He had one thing to say.
He didn't go into details of how he ended up this way,
Suffice to say that he and his dog no longer had somewhere to stay,
And though it broke his heart in two, the old man had to admit
That as much as he loved that chihuahua, there was no way he could care for him.
But he knew that the young man could, so he packed up the cart and rolled over
And he planned to abandon his beloved dog on the steps of that three story condo.

But since he saw the young man was awake, the old man revised his plan,
And instead of leaving the dog alone, he put him right in the young man's hands.
"Please take care of my dog, I wish I could take him with me.
But he'll be so happy here, as a part of your beautiful family."
And that was all that he said because he didn't want to cry,
As he walked back to his shopping cart and rattled off into the night.
But that chihuahua erupted. He whimpered, cried, and

barked.
And he leapt right out of the young man's hands, and chased the shopping cart.

The old man heard the dog, he scooped him up and he kissed him.
He tried to say goodbye again, but the chihuahua refused to listen.
The young man said, "I want that dog, I'll admit that much is true,
But ain't no way in hell I could come between that dog and you."
And he reached back for his wallet for a twenty dollar bill.
He told the old man keep it for when the doggie needs meals,
But the old man refused this money, and the chihuahua hopped back atop
The rattling shopping cart as it disappeared into the dark.

Chapter 12: The Reason

There were two silver rails running side by side
They were mostly invisible in the dead of the night
Until headlights reflected as they train made its way from
The empty platforms of the empty train stations.
But at one of the stations, an old main was waiting
For the last train leaving the station to take him
Back home again where his wife waits for him.

The old man heard the train's distant rumble,
Saw the tracks light up leading out of the tunnel,
He didn't have much time left to savor
The things that he loved but he couldn't take with him.
And all that came down to the little chihuahua
Perched up top of his shopping cart and
The old man offered him one final snuggle
Called him a good boy and told him he loved him.

And then set him down on the cold tile ground.
The chihuahua watched the old man turn around,
And walk to the edge of the train platform.
The dog started barking, trying to warn him.
A train was coming! The old man had to stop!
But the old man ignored him and continued to walk.
The train horn screamed out a murderous threat.
The headlights saw the old man's silhouette.

The chihuahua could not bark loud enough,
So he latched onto the old man's pants cuff,
And he tugged and he pulled with all of his soul.
The old man tried to walk, but the doggie kept hold,
And the tiny weight of that little chihuahua
Was an anchor that stopped all the old man's progress.
Backwards he fell onto the tiles
As all the train cars blew safely by him.

The old man realized that he had been conquered
By the tiny little Chihuahua that was now sitting right on top of him.
He was eye to eye with that angry little doggie,
But he heard him as clearly as if he were talking.

He said you matter to me.
Your love is still needed.
You don't want to die.
Let me be the reason.

The old man climbed off off the dirty old tile floor,
And returned to his shopping cart once more,
And up on top, the little Chihuahua hopped,
And the two rattled off and disappeared into the dark.